This book belongs to:

_____

My Christmas Collection

The Legend of
the Three Trees

Santa, Are You
For Real?

The Tiny Star

Three Favorite Stories

Tommy NELSON®

A Division of Thomas Nelson Publishers
Since 1798

www.thomasnelson.com

The Legend of the Three Trees from the screenplay by George Taweel and Rob Loos is based on the traditional folk tale.
Text and illustrations copyright © 2001 by Tommy Nelson®, a Division of Thomas Nelson, Inc.
Story adapted by Catherine McCafferty
Illustrations by Vaccaro Associates
Published in Nashville, Tennessee, by Tommy Nelson®, a Division of Thomas Nelson, Inc.

Santa, Are You For Real?
Text copyright © 1979, 1997 by Harold Myra
Illustrations copyright © 1997 by Tommy Nelson®, a Division of Thomas Nelson, Inc.
Published in Nashville, Tennessee, by Tommy Nelson®, a Division of Thomas Nelson, Inc.
Scripture quotations are from the *International Children's Bible*®, *New Century Version*®, © 1986, 1988, 1999 by Tommy Nelson®, a Division of Thomas Nelson, Inc.

The Tiny Star
Text copyright © 1989, 1997 by Arthur Ginolfi
Illustrations copyright © 1989, 1997 by Pat Schories
Scripture quotations are from the *International Children's Bible*®, *New Century Version*®, © 1986, 1988, 1999 by Tommy Nelson®, a Division of Thomas Nelson, Inc.

ISBN-13: 978-1-4003-0843-9
ISBN-10: 1-4003-0843-7

Printed in China
06 07 08 09 10 TWP 9 8 7 6 5 4 3 2 1

The Legend
of the

Three

Trees

From the screenplay by

George Taweel and Rob Loos,

based on the traditional folk tale

adaptation by Catherine McCafferty

as by Gene 'n Geppy Productions

Life burst into the world on the third day of Creation. From under the water, God brought forth the earth. Peeking up through the earth's soil, green plants waved like millions of tiny flags. Grasses, bushes, and trees grew into every size and shape.

The trees towered above all. There were pine trees and poplar, olive and oak, willow and walnut. Each held its own seeds and fruits.

Their seeds and fruits scattered as animals carried them from the trees. In a green valley, a fox dropped an olive pit. From that pit, a new olive tree with beautiful wood began to grow.

Along a rocky shoreline, a stork dropped an acorn into a deep crack. From that acorn, a great oak tree began to grow.

High on a mountainside, a clumsy goat
knocked a log into a tree. The crash sent pine
cones and their seeds spinning to the ground.
From one of those seeds, a new pine tree
began to grow.

Each of the trees had great dreams of what it would become.

The olive tree hoped that its beautiful wood could become a treasure chest. Decorated with sparkling jewels, it would hold the greatest treasure in the world.

The oak hoped to become a mighty ship.

Strong and proud, it would carry kings
and queens across the waters.

The tall, majestic pine hoped that its towering branches would remind people of the glory of God's Creation. It dreamed that it would always stay on the mountain and point people to God.

Many years passed. The trees' dreams had not come true.
The olive tree had become a simple manger for feeding animals.

The mighty oak's wood was made into a little fishing boat.

And the great pine fell in a storm and lay in a heap of old lumber.

But God had His own plan for each of the trees.

One night, shepherds keeping watch over their flock saw an angel. A great light shone all around. The angel told them not to be afraid, for their Savior had been born in Bethlehem. Just as the angel had said, the shepherds found the baby lying in a manger.

The olive tree had not become a treasure chest, but now, as a manger, it held the greatest treasure of all time—God's only Son, Jesus.

The infant Jesus grew into a man and traveled to the very lake that held the oak fishing boat. One day, the little boat carried Jesus onto the lake with the fishermen. Suddenly, a great storm swept over the lake. The oak boat struggled with all of its strength so it would not sink.

"Quiet! Be still," Jesus said. The storm stopped. The oak boat felt Jesus' power. The boat had never carried a king of this world. But now it carried the King of Kings!

One day, soldiers came for the forgotten pine. From the pine's trunk, they made a cross and they placed Jesus on it. Under a blackening sky, the pine cross swayed as the soldiers raised it. The cross did not know if it could bear the weight of the man upon it. But it did.

That day, Jesus died on the cross to take away the sins of all who believe in Him. And ever since, the cross points people to God as a symbol of His great love for us.

Sometimes, the dreams that we have for ourselves are much smaller than the dreams that God has for us. The three trees' dreams came true, just not in the way they imagined.

And so it is with each of us. For if we follow God's path, we will travel far beyond even our greatest dreams.

Santa,
Are You For Real?

Harold Myra

ILLUSTRATED BY JANE KURISU

'Twas the night before Christmas,
and out on the street,
a wee boy was standing,
big boots on his feet.

He stamped them and kicked them,
threw snow at a rock
to crowd out the songs
of the kids on the block.

"Hey, hey, hey," he heard them say,
"Santa's phony—all the way!
Hey! No way, a flying sleigh!"

Dad watched Todd come in,
saw his face was all glum,
so he bent down and asked,
"What's the matter,
old chum?"

"No Santa or reindeer will
come to our place!
The chimney's too skinny.
He can't really fly.
He's not at the North Pole.
It's all a big lie."

Dad reached for the boy,
pulled him tight to his side,
and kissed him and told him,
"Let's see, Todd, who's lied."

Saint Nicholas was a real person.
He lived about 300 years after
Jesus was born. He loved
Jesus very much.

One favorite story about
him goes like this:

*Nicholas loved to give gifts,
especially to the poor.
Only he gave them
secretly because
he wasn't looking
for thanks.*

Nick knew a kind but poor man with three lovely daughters who all wanted to get married. But in those days, a woman had to have money—a dowry—before a wedding could be announced.

When Nick heard about this, he put some money into a bag and, while it was dark, walked to their house.

He tossed the money into the oldest daughter's room, and it fell into a stocking hung there to dry. Nick quietly left.

The oldest daughter had a marvelous wedding.

Later, on another night, Nick did the same thing for the second daughter.

But who had helped them? they wondered.

One daughter was left. Would someone give her a dowry too?

Not too long after that Nick sneaked up to her house and tossed in a third bag of gold. But this time the father heard him! Nick realized he had been seen and tried to dash away. But the father ran and caught up to him.

The father recognized Nick and smiled.

"Keep my secret," Nick asked.

And the father did.

For years after that, no one knew who had helped the three daughters.

And because Nick loved Jesus, he kept doing kind things for people.

After he died, people called him a saint.

And over the years, people remembered Saint Nicholas and how he gave gifts.

In Holland they call him Sinterclaas. In England they call him Father Christmas. In France he is called Père Nöel. In the United States he is called Santa Claus.

The real Saint Nicholas is now in heaven with Jesus. When you see a Santa in a store or a parade, think of Saint Nick.

Of course some children know all about Santa and presents and reindeer but forget all about Jesus. For Saint Nick, that would ruin Christmas! Jesus was Nick's whole life.

Saint Nicholas gave gifts because Jesus came on the first Christmas to give himself for us.

Todd said, "I'm going
to do what Nick was about,
I'm going to give gifts
and not be found out!"

Todd ran up the stairs,
his face full of scheming.
A long time went by
till he came back all beaming.

Stuffed toys and a dump truck,
a clown with one leg
all wrapped for Michelle
and her brother Greg.

Todd piled them up high
by the tree lighted bright,
and then he announced,
"Saint Nick's here tonight!"

"I'll act like Saint Nick," Todd said to his dad.
"It's Jesus he loved—He makes us all glad!"

His dad just laughed as he lifted the boy.
"That's wonderful, Todd.
To share gives us joy."

As the family sat around
and talked half the night,
Todd thought he saw,
in the snow and
moonlight . . .

. . . a bright-eyed Saint Nicholas
with his sack looking in,
and wide across his face,
a jolly old grin.

The Tiny Star

The Greatest Star the World Has Ever Seen!

Arthur Ginolfi

Illustrated by Pat Schories

A very long time ago there was a tiny star named Starlet.

She was so small she could hardly be seen. All the other stars were much bigger and brighter than Starlet.

At night when people looked up at the sky,
they saw all the big, bright stars.

But no one ever saw Starlet.

One night Starlet asked the other stars if there was some way she could twinkle and sparkle like them. But the stars just laughed and said, "Oh, no, Starlet. You are far too small." Starlet felt very sad, and she began to cry. "No one ever sees me," she said. "I wish I were bigger."

Later that night the wise old moon looked at Starlet.

"Why are you so sad?" he asked.

"Because," said Starlet, "I try to twinkle and sparkle, but I am the smallest star in the sky, and no one ever sees me."

"Don't be sad," said the old moon gently. "How big or small you are is not important. Someday, somewhere someone will see you."

"But when?" asked Starlet.

The moon smiled and said, "Someday, somewhere." And he went on his way.

Many years passed. Night after night Starlet shone,
but no one ever saw her. Then one night Starlet began
to fall from the sky! Down, down, down she fell.

Starlet landed gently on the roof of a little stable.

Everything was dark and quiet. The only sounds she heard were those of the animals.

Then Starlet heard a baby crying!

Starlet looked inside the stable and saw a newborn baby lying in a manger.

"Oh!" she cried. "This stable is so cold and dark. Perhaps I can shine enough to brighten it up."

So Starlet moved closer to the baby. When the baby saw Starlet and felt the warmth of her gentle rays, he began to smile. The more the baby smiled, the brighter Starlet shone!

The whole stable glowed. It was a miracle.

As Starlet grew brighter, she began to rise. Up, up, up into the sky, higher and higher, brighter and brighter. Starlet was now the brightest star in the sky. Everyone saw the magnificent star. This was the moment she had always wished for!

And on that special night, shining over the little stable in Bethlehem, Starlet was the most beautiful star the world had ever seen.

"I am the light of the world.
The person who follows me will never
live in darkness.
He will have the light that gives life."

—John 8:12
ICB